NICOLAS FRUCTUS

THORINTH

#1 THE FOOL WITH NO NAME

Humanoids Publishing ™

www.humanoids-publishing.com

Translation by Justin Kelly

Graphic design & lettering: Thierry Frissen

THORINTH #1: THE FOOL WITH NO NAME

English language edition © 2002 Humanoids Inc. Los Angeles, CA, USA.
All rights reserved.

Humanoids Publishing
PO Box 931658
Hollywood, CA 90093

Printed and bound in Belgium.

ISBN: 1-930652-28-3

Humanoids Publishing™ and the Humanoids Publishing logo are trademarks of:
Les Humanoïdes Associés S.A., Geneva (Switzerland)
registered in various categories and countries.
Humanoids Publishing, a division of Humanoids Group.

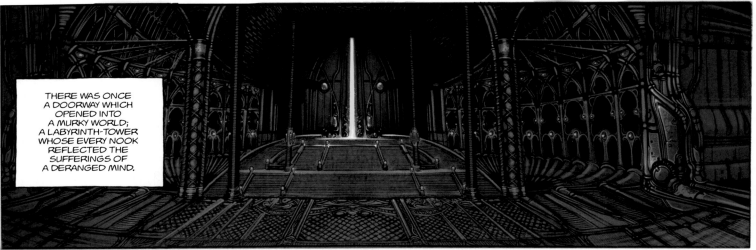

THERE WAS ONCE
A DOORWAY WHICH
OPENED INTO
A MURKY WORLD;
A LABYRINTH-TOWER
WHOSE EVERY NOOK
REFLECTED THE
SUFFERINGS OF
A DERANGED MIND.

TO ENTER,
ONE HAD ONLY TO
STAND ON ITS
THRESHOLD AND
WAIT FOR
ADMITTANCE.

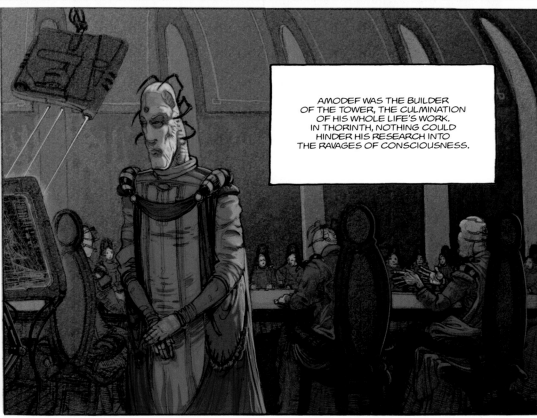

AMODEF WAS THE BUILDER
OF THE TOWER, THE CULMINATION
OF HIS WHOLE LIFE'S WORK.
IN THORINTH, NOTHING COULD
HINDER HIS RESEARCH INTO
THE RAVAGES OF CONSCIOUSNESS.

FOUNDER OF THE CLAN OF
BRAIN SURGEONS KNOWN
AS THE PELLEGENS, AMODEF
LAID THE FIRST STONE OF
THORINTH, PAVING THE WAY
TO AN UNDERSTANDING
OF THE HUMAN MIND.

FAMILIAR WITH THE MIND'S TRICKS AND TURNS, AMODEF KNEW HE'D BE ABLE TO PENETRATE UNKNOWN GATEWAYS AND REACH PLACES NOT YET ATTAINED.

BUT THE SUCCESS OF ONE CAN OFTEN BE THE ENVY OF ANOTHER. THE MASTER ARCHITECT, ESIATH, TAILORED THE TOWER'S CONSTRUCTION TO SUIT HER PLANS. THORINTH WOULD BE HER GREATEST WORK AND HER MEANS OF DOMINATION.

SHE POSITIONED A MASS OF FLOATING CLAY AT THE VERY CENTER OF THORINTH...

...AND HID IT FROM AMODEF, UNTIL THE TOWER WAS COMPLETE.

AMODEF WAS STUNNED WHEN HE SAW THE MASSIVE BLOCK. SO ESIATH EXTOLLED ITS VIRTUES FOR HIS THERAPEUTIC RESEARCH. IT REQUIRED A GOOD DOSE OF IMAGINATION.

2

AMODEF WAS DISPLEASED BY THIS DEVELOPMENT, BUT ESIATH CONVINCED HIM TO GATHER THE PELLEGEN AROUND THE MASS SO THAT SHE COULD SHOW THEM THE TRUE NATURE OF HER CREATION.

THE MUTATED CLAY, SHAPED BY INVISIBLE HANDS, HAD THE POWER TO SHOW HER THOUGHTS. ESIATH HAD PIONEERED ARCHITECTURE OF THE MIND.

STEP RIGHT UP, DOCTORS! DO YOU NOT WISH TO SEE WHAT HAUNTS YOUR SPIRITS? I NOW OFFER WHAT YOU HAVE ALWAYS DREAMED. DO YOU NOT WISH TO READ IN THIS MIRROR THE THOUGHTS THAT HAVE BEEN WRITTEN BEHIND YOUR EYES?

MY DEAR AMODEF, YOU APPEAR SO RESERVED BEFORE THIS GREAT DISCOVERY... JEALOUSY, PERHAPS? ...OR MERELY FRUSTRATED PRIDE?

THE PRIDE OF HAVING A TOWER BUILT TO STUDY WHAT HAS ALREADY BEEN SOLVED BY AN ARCHITECTURAL ALCHEMIST?

3

ESIATH'S BRILLIANCE DIDN'T END THERE. HER ARCHITECTURE OF THE MIND WAS DESTINED FOR OTHER AIMS INDEED.

SHE WAITED UNTIL THE PELLEGEN WERE SUFFICIENTLY IMPRESSED BY THE CLAY'S ABILITIES...

...UNTIL NOTHING COULD STAND BEFORE HER POWER.

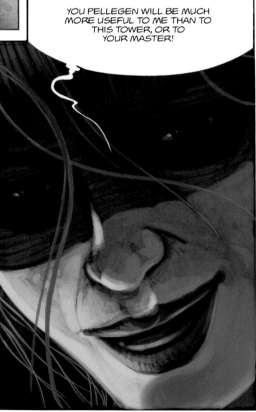

YOU PELLEGEN WILL BE MUCH MORE USEFUL TO ME THAN TO THIS TOWER, OR TO YOUR MASTER!

THEN, CONCENTRATING ONCE MORE, ESIATH REVERSED THE CLAY'S ENERGY. FAR FROM BEING A MIRROR TO THEIR THOUGHTS, THE CLAY ABSORBED THE DOCTORS' MINDS...

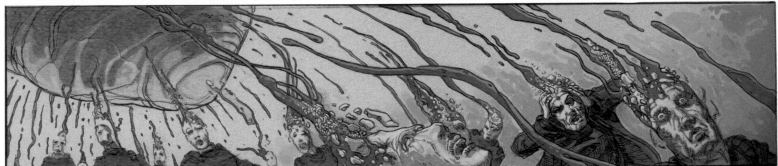

ESIATH HAD CREATED A GOLEM, A CREATURE TO HELP HER RULE THE TOWER. NOW, THE KNOWLEDGE OF THOSE WHO SEARCH MEN'S SOULS WAS IMPRISONED WITHIN THAT CLAY ...

...CONTAINED IN A SERVILE BEING, HER ALL-POWERFUL ENFORCER...

ALL YOU NEED NOW IS A BODY, WHICH I GIVE YOU...

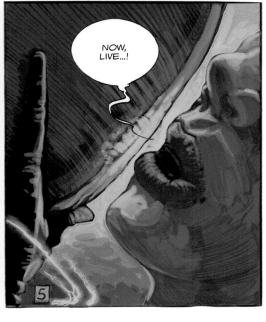

NOW, LIVE...!

5

ESIATH NEVER HAD THE CHANCE TO BEHOLD HER CREATION. IN HIS OWN WAY, HER FOOL-KEEPER GAVE HER A LAST KISS...

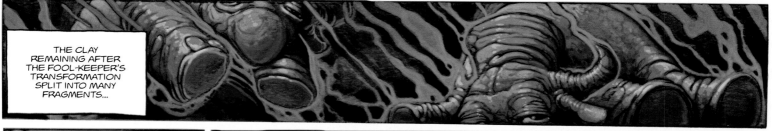

THE CLAY REMAINING AFTER THE FOOL-KEEPER'S TRANSFORMATION SPLIT INTO MANY FRAGMENTS...

...AND EACH OF THOSE TINY FRAGMENTS BECAME A SCHNUBBIT.

AMODEF, THE SLAUGHTER'S SOLE SURVIVOR, BORE THE FULL BRUNT OF THE NEWBORN SCHNUBBITS' CRAWLING, CHATTERING MASS.

6

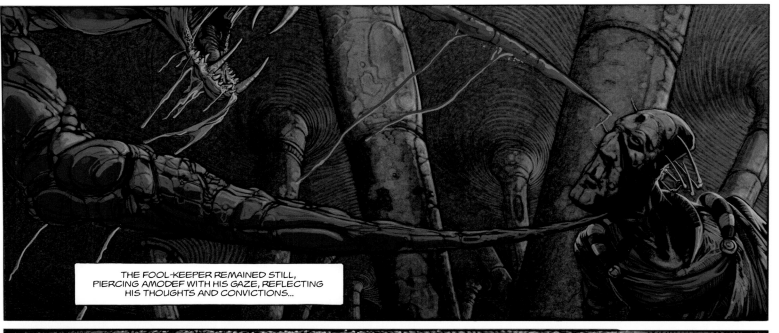

THE FOOL-KEEPER REMAINED STILL,
PIERCING AMODEF WITH HIS GAZE, REFLECTING
HIS THOUGHTS AND CONVICTIONS...

THEN THE FOOL-KEEPER
DEPARTED, VANISHING
INTO THE TUNNELS OF
THORINTH. AND THE
SCHNUBBITS SCATTERED,
LEAVING AMODEF ALONE
IN THE AFTERMATH...

THEY SAY THE FOOL-KEEPER LIVES NOWHERE.
HE ONLY EXISTS WHEN HE ACTS. BUT THE SCHNUBBITS
ARE EVERYWHERE. THEY ARE THE GUIDES.
THEY SAY THEY'RE THE ONLY ONES WHO CAN SPEAK
TO THE FOOL-KEEPER. NOBODY HAS HAD THE
COURAGE TO TRY OTHERWISE...

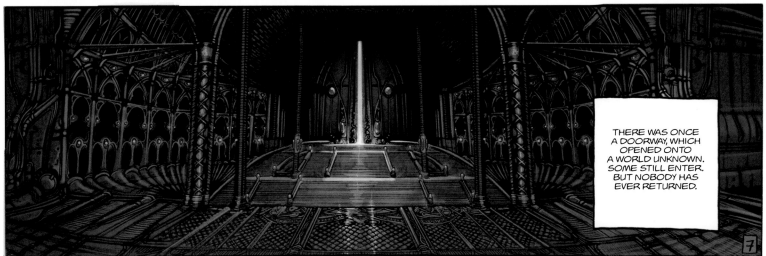

THERE WAS ONCE
A DOORWAY, WHICH
OPENED ONTO
A WORLD UNKNOWN.
SOME STILL ENTER.
BUT NOBODY HAS
EVER RETURNED.

7

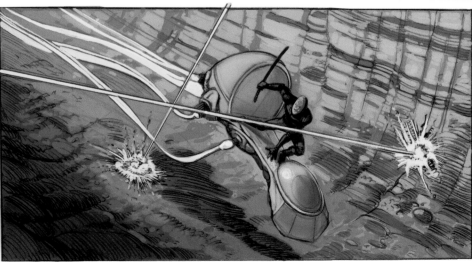

YOU WON'T DIE. I AIMED TO MISS YOUR HEART.

RETURN TO YOUR SUPERIORS AND TELL THEM NOTHING WILL STOP ME FROM ENTERING THORINTH.

YOU... YOU WON'T GET IN. AND YOU'LL NEVER GET YOUR WIFE OUT, EITHER. SHE BELONGS IN THE TOWER, NOT OUT HERE.

ALSO TELL THEM THAT AFTER I'VE FREED HER FROM THORINTH, I'LL HUNT DOWN THOSE WHO TOOK HER THERE, ONE BY ONE...

FAREWELL.

10

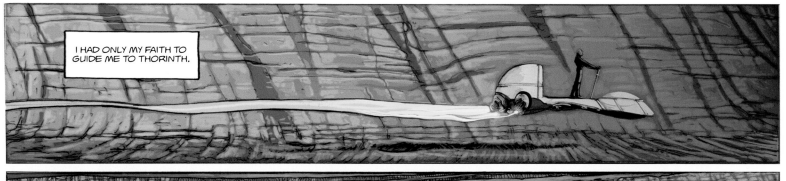

I HAD ONLY MY FAITH TO GUIDE ME TO THORINTH.

SUCH RECKLESSNESS IS REQUIRED WHEN THEY TAKE AWAY EVERYTHING YOUR LIFE WAS BUILT ON.

THORINTH, THE INTERIOR WORLD FROM WHICH NOBODY EVER EMERGES. THE PERFECT PLACE TO BANISH MADALIS TEMROTH.

OUTSIDE, SHE MADE THEM AFRAID. "HER RESEARCH IS TOO DANGEROUS," SAID THE MOST FEARFUL ONES.

MADALIS PAID NO
HEED. SHE WORKED
HARDER, PUSHING
HER RESEARCH
FURTHER AHEAD.

THEIR
RESPONSE
WAS SWIFT AND
SURE. HER
DETRACTORS
WASTED NO
TIME IN
EXILING HER
TO THORINTH.

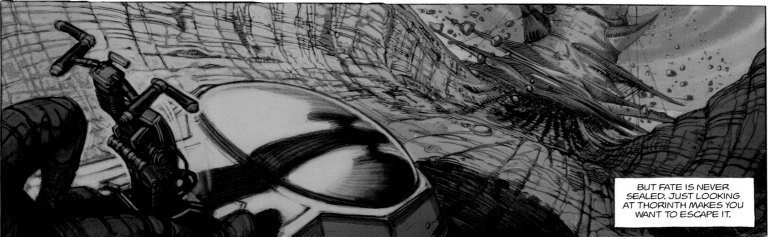

BUT FATE IS NEVER
SEALED. JUST LOOKING
AT THORINTH MAKES YOU
WANT TO ESCAPE IT.

13

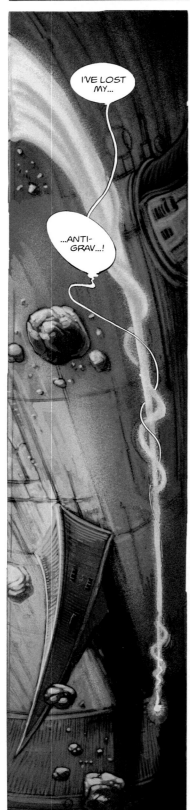

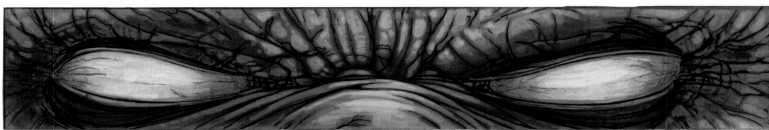

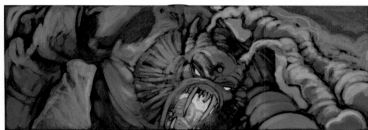

16

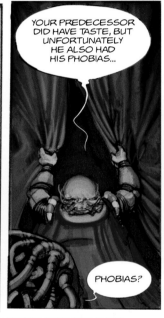

DON'T TOUCH... THE POINT... YOUNG MAN. DEADLY... POISON.

WHO WAS IT?

A SANODATH! IT'S IMPOSSIBLE TO STOP HIM!

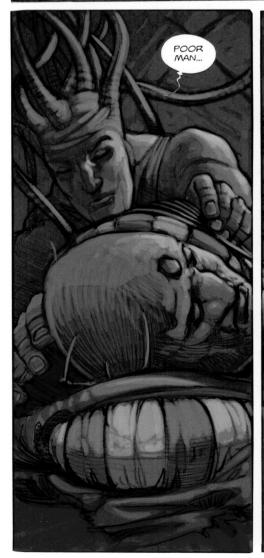

POOR MAN...

WHY KILL SUCH A FRIENDLY PELLEGEN...?

WHAT?! ON THE POINT...

...IT'S THE EMBLEM OF MADALIS!

YOUR WIFE KILLED HIM?

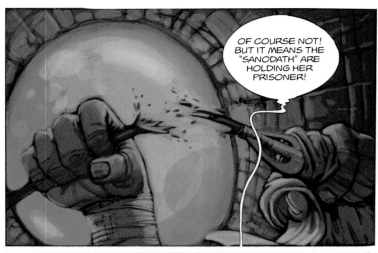

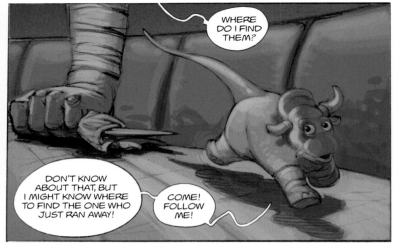

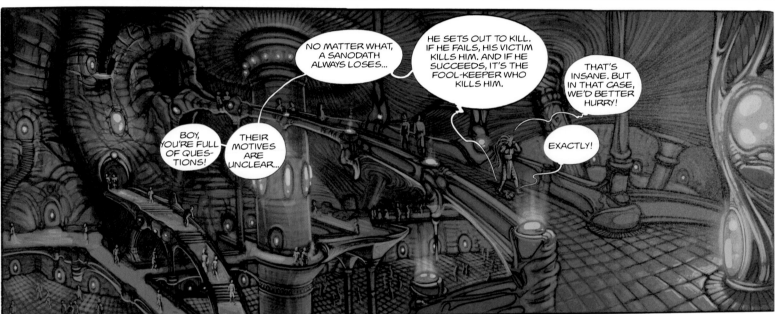

I'M PLEASED TO SEE YOU ON YOUR FEET SO SOON. JOIN US...

WELL, I... OKAY.

BARKEEP! ANOTHER ROUND!

HELLO!

DON'T BE OFFENDED, MY BOY... THEY'RE MEDITATORS. RATHER CONTEMPLA-TIVE... BUT GOOD CONVERSATIONALISTS, DON'T YOU KNOW.

I SEE...

PLEASED TO...

YES, LIKEWISE!

DON'T BE OFFENDED, MY BOY... SHE'S...

IT'S OKAY, REALLY...

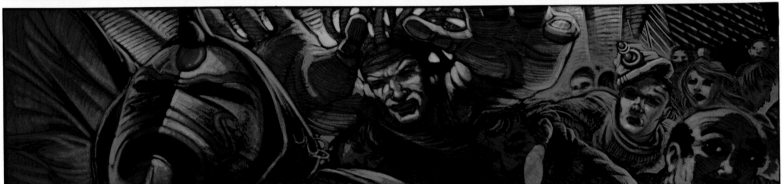

30

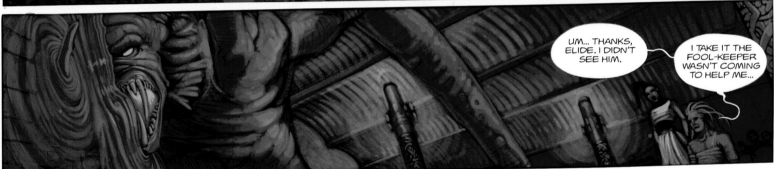

EXCUSE ME, BUT... COULD YOU PLEASE LEAVE THE TAVERN? NOTHING AGAINST YOU, BUT CUSTOMERS WON'T DARE COME IN WITH YOU HERE.

YES, I SEE. I'LL GET MY THINGS AND LEAVE.

THANKS.

I'LL WAIT OUTSIDE.

I'LL BE RIGHT THERE!

THE TROUBLE WITH THE FOOL-KEEPER IS THAT HE DISINTEGRATES ALL THE CLUES.

WHAT'S BEHIND THE CURTAIN?

WHAT A MESS...

THERE! BY THE BENCH!

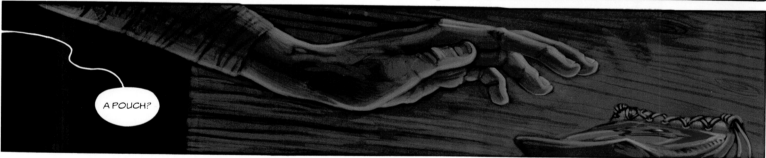

A POUCH?

MADALIS' EMBLEM! AGAIN?

LET'S FIND ELIDE. WE'LL FIGURE THIS OUT LATER.

WITH PLEASURE! ALL THIS HAS WORN ME OUT.

A MALFUNC-
TIONING
CRAFT...

THE VANISHING
CORPSE OF A
PELLEGEN...

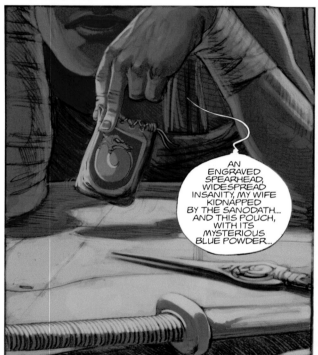

AN
ENGRAVED
SPEARHEAD,
WIDESPREAD
INSANITY, MY WIFE
KIDNAPPED
BY THE SANODATH...
AND THIS POUCH,
WITH ITS
MYSTERIOUS
BLUE POWDER...

HMM... IN A WAY, IT'S
REASSURING. MADALIS
MUST STILL BE ALIVE,
EVEN IF SHE IS IN THE
CLUTCHES OF THOSE
SUICIDAL MANIACS...

I HAVE TO FIGURE OUT
WHAT THIS POWDER'S
FOR, THEN FIND THE LAIR
OF THE SANODATH.

HEY,
WAKE UP!
DO YOU KNOW
WHAT THIS
BLUE
POWDER'S
FOR?

I CAN'T EVEN
GET FIVE
MINUTES'
REST!

WAIT...
THAT'S...!

HEY!!!

36

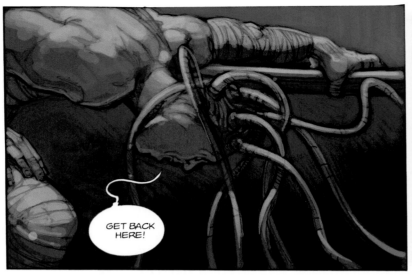

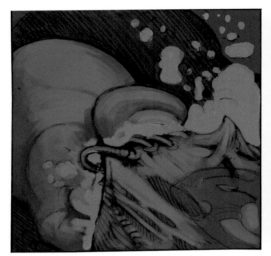

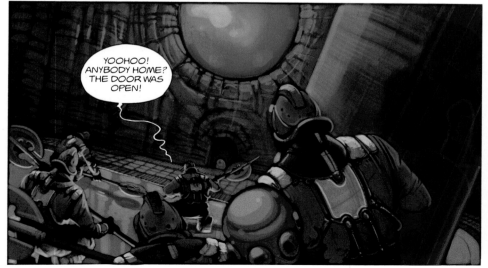

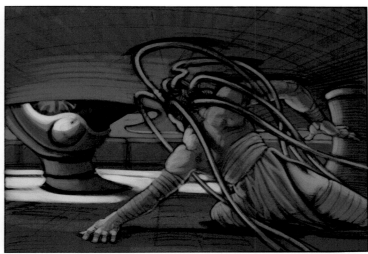

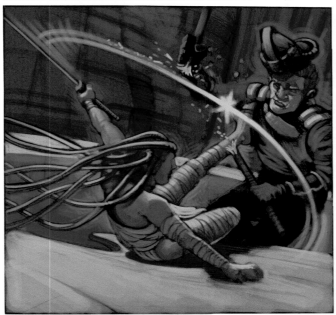

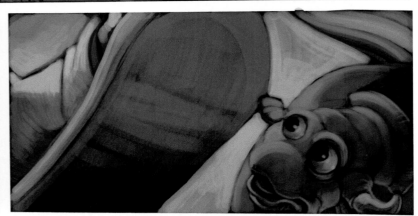

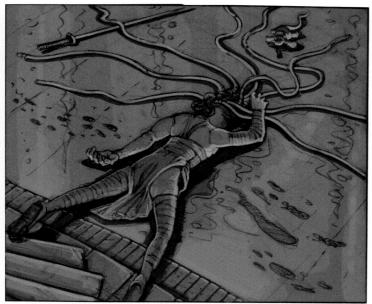

YOUR PRESIDENCY, IT GIVES ME GREAT HONOR TO INTRODUCE OUR PLAINTIFF, THE SO-CALLED KING, WHOSE CHARGES HAVE CONSEQUENCES THAT CONCERN US ALL!

WHAT DO YOU MEAN, "SO-CALLED KING"? I'M THE KING! THAT'S FINAL!

THAT'S RIGHT, LADIES AND GENTLEMEN! SINCE ENTERING THE TOWER, THE NEWCOMER HAS UNSCRUPULOUSLY VIOLATED ALL OUR LAWS AND CAUSED SEVERE DAMAGE!

NOT TO MENTION THE FACT THAT HE IS ABNORMALLY NORMAL! BY PELLEGEN CUSTOM, NORMALITY IS A GREAT CRIME! HIS PRESENCE IS SACRILEGE!

AND THAT'S NOT ALL! HE HAS JOINED FORCES WITH THE SANODATH, WHO FOR THE LAST SEVERAL CYCLES HAVE PLOTTED TO HUNT PELLEGEN! HIS FIRST ACT WAS TO MURDER ONE OF OUR CLAN!

WE ADMIRE YOU GREATLY, GRAND ACCUSER. HOWEVER... COULD WE PLEASE GET TO THE FACTS?

YES! SHOW THE EVIDENCE, THEN LYNCH HIM!

AHEM... RIGHT AWAY, YOUR PRESIDENCY!

LET'S FINISH THIS!

HEAR, HEAR!

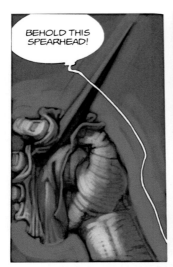

BEHOLD THIS SPEARHEAD!

WE FOUND IT ON HIS PERSON! WE ARE NOT IN THE PRESENCE OF A MADMAN, BUT A KILLER WHO TAKES PLEASURE IN RETRIEVING THE MURDER WEAPON, LIKE A TROPHY!

INDECENT!

GHASTLY!

IMAGINE HOW HE MUST HAVE TRADED HIS PSYCHOSIS FOR THE MACABRE DELIGHT OF KILLING THE VERY MAN WHO CURED HIM!

THIS IS AWFUL! THEY'RE SAYING HE ISN'T CRAZY!

HE'S DONE FOR...

THAT'S IT!

ENOUGH EVIDENCE! LET'S KILL HIM!

THERE'S ALSO THIS SMALL POUCH OF DRUGS, HALF-CONSUMED...

HE'S RIGHT!

...WHICH PROVES HE SNORTED IT TO ENTER HIS KILLING FRENZY!

SHOCKING! WHAT SAYS THE ACCUSED?

THAT CLINCHES IT!

HURRY UP AND EXECUTE HIM!

WHAT NEXT?

HOW HORRIBLE!

EVIDENCE DOESN'T MATTER WHEN THERE'S BEEN MURDER!

THERE'S ONLY ONE OPTION!

THANK YOU FOR YOUR KIND ATTENTION. I WILL ENDEAVOR TO BE BRIEF. I HAVE SPOKEN BEFORE YOU WITH NO JOY IN MY HEART, BUT RATHER WEIGHED DOWN BY THE SAD

WE'VE SEEN ENOUGH!

GET RID OF HIM!

BLOOD FOR BLOOD! IT'S THE ONLY WAY!

TORTURE HIM!

LISTEN TO HIM! HE'S LYING!

NOW THAT THE ACCUSED HAS HAD HIS SAY, PLEASE GO ON, GRAND ACCUSER. SILENCE, IF YOU PLEASE!

THANK YOU, YOUR PRESIDENCY! I WILL CONCLUDE WITH ONE FINAL NOTE!

HERE'S THE WEAPON HE WOULD HAVE USED TO DECAPITATE THE PELLEGEN!

SO?

WE KNOW ALREADY!

THE SANODATH RECENTLY BEGAN CHOPPING OFF HEADS AND ONLY NOW HAVE WE RECOVERED A BLADE!

BUT THE ACCUSED HAD NO TIME TO DECAPITATE THE GOOD DOCTOR! HE HAD TO RUSH TO THE TAVERN, TO SECURE AN ALIBI IN THE PRESENCE OF THE KING!

DECAPITATION... HOW STRANGE. WHY THE OVERKILL?

WHAT SAYS THE ACCUSED?

MY HEAD! ...NOT AGAIN!

SEE? MORE PROOF! HE'S BOWED DOWN BY GUILT!

I'LL TRY...

THE FOOL-KEEPER!

EXCUSE ME!

I SEE THE POUCH! KEEP DISTRACTING HIM!

GOT IT! GOT IT!!

HURRY!

48

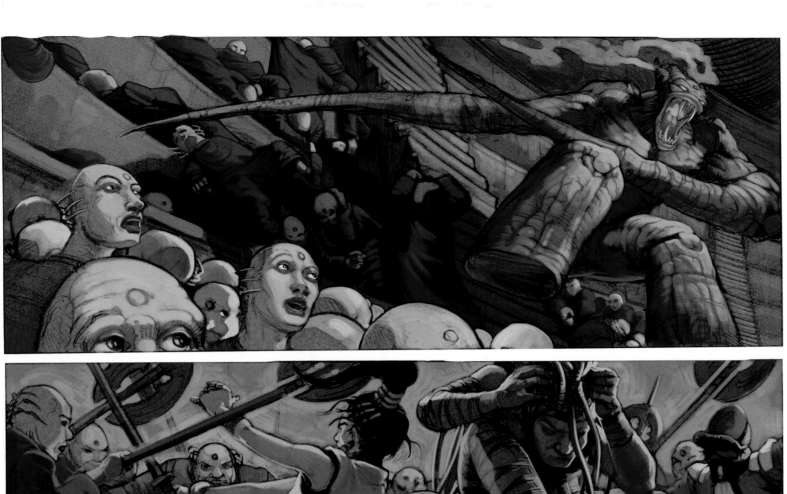

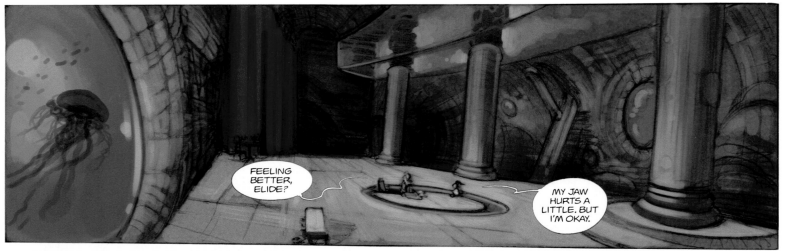

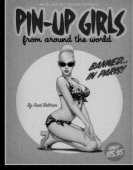